The hardest part of any magic show is picking the right assistant.

Not everyone is a born performer.

Some suffer from stage fright,

while others have a terrible sense of timing.

And not everyone understands props.

But Houdini the rabbit was a natural.

He **loved** magic.

And he had a knack for bringing the team together.

From the after-show treats,

to the pre-show
checks,

EUCH!

Houdini took care of everyone and everything.

So one night,
when things
went wrong...

Houdini carried on with the show.

The crowd thought it was the best trick **ever.**

But the magician wasn't too pleased...

when they discovered his new role might be permanent.

As rehearsals got underway, not everyone was impressed by Houdini's talent.

NOM...

And their new boss seemed far too busy.

INTRODUCING...

HOUDINI

But word soon spread.

Houdini's hard work began to pay off
as people flocked to see the show.

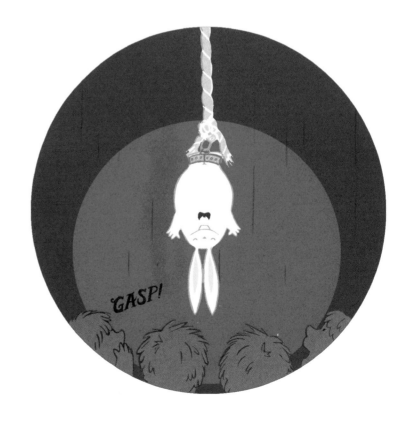

TICK
TICK
TICK

The more daring
his tricks became,
the more the crowd
loved him.

Houdini was a hit.

TADAA

HOORAY!

GASP!

Night after night the audience cheered.

Clap CLAP CLAP CLAP clap CLAP CLAP clap CLAP clap clap clap CLAP CLAP clap CLAP CLAP Clap Clap CLAP CLAP CLAP Clap Clap CLAP CLAP CLAP CLAP clap clap CLAP

But for Houdini, the
excitement was fading.

Though he'd enjoyed his time in the spotlight,

someone else needed it more.

So he gathered
the team together.
On the last night of his
sell-out tour, Houdini
would attempt...

his greatest trick.

SHA

TADAAA!
TADAA!
TADAA!
Tadaa
WOOHOO!
ORAY!
CLAP
GASP!
CLAP
CLAP
CLAP

Which goes to show

that sometimes rabbits
(and people)

do the most unexpected things...

because life is **truly** magical when you share it.

FEATURING
HOUDINI
AND THE
HOPPERS

SOLD OUT

STAGE
DOOR

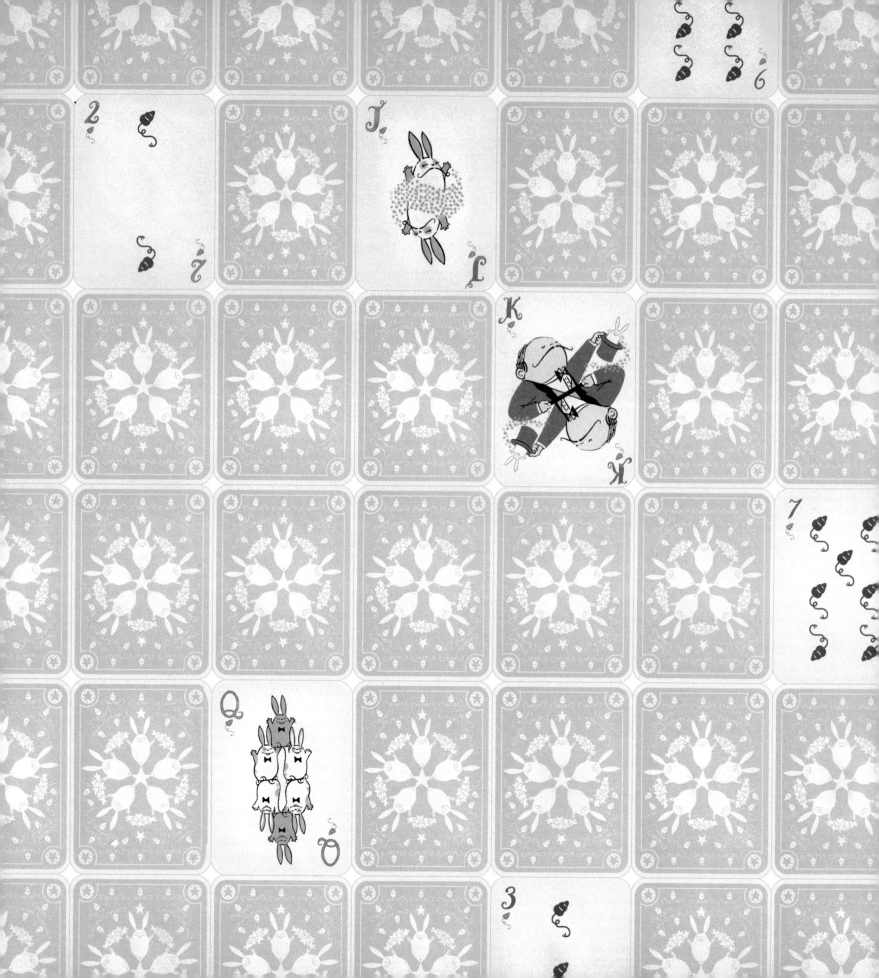